THE NIGHT BEFORE CHRISTMAS

For Sushila and next Christmas – R.J.

THE NIGHT BEFORE CHRISTMAS

CLEMENT CLARKE MOORE
Illustrated by Richard Johnson

PICTURE CORGI

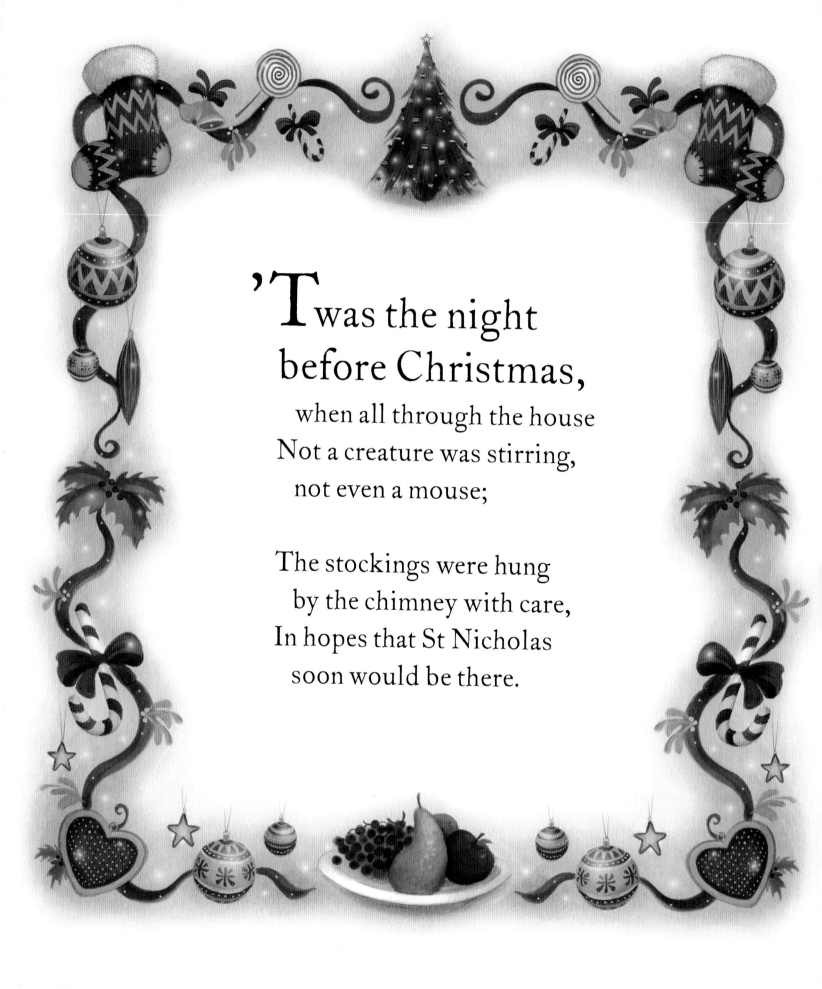

'Twas the night
before Christmas,
when all through the house
Not a creature was stirring,
not even a mouse;

The stockings were hung
by the chimney with care,
In hopes that St Nicholas
soon would be there.

The children were nestled all snug in their beds,
While visions of sugarplums danced in their heads;

And Mama in her kerchief, and I in my cap,
Had just settled our brains for a long winter's nap—

When out on the lawn
   there arose such a clatter,
I sprang from the bed
   to see what was the matter.

Away to the window
   I flew like a flash,
Tore open the shutters
   and threw up the sash.

The moon on the breast of the new-fallen snow
Gave the lustre of midday to objects below;
When, what to my wondering eyes should appear,
But a miniature sleigh, and eight tiny reindeer,

With a little old driver,
   so lively and quick,
I knew in a moment
   it must be St Nick.

More rapid than eagles
   his coursers they came,
And he whistled, and shouted,
   and called them by name:

"Now, Dasher! Now, Dancer! Now, Prancer and Vixen!
On, Comet! On, Cupid! On, Donner and Blitzen!
To the top of the porch! To the top of the wall!
Now dash away! Dash away! Dash away all!"

As dry leaves that before
the wild hurricane fly,
When they meet with an obstacle,
mount to the sky;

So up to the house-top
the coursers they flew,
With the sleigh full of toys –
and St Nicholas too.

And then in a twinkling, I heard on the roof
The prancing and pawing of each little hoof –

As I drew in my head, and was turning around,
Down the chimney St Nicholas came with a bound.

He was dressed all in fur, from his head to his foot,
And his clothes were all tarnished with ashes and soot;
A bundle of toys he had flung on his back,
And he looked like a pedlar just opening his pack.

His eyes – how they twinkled!
His dimples: how merry!
His cheeks were like roses,
his nose like a cherry!

His droll little mouth
was drawn up like a bow,
And the beard of his chin
was as white as the snow!

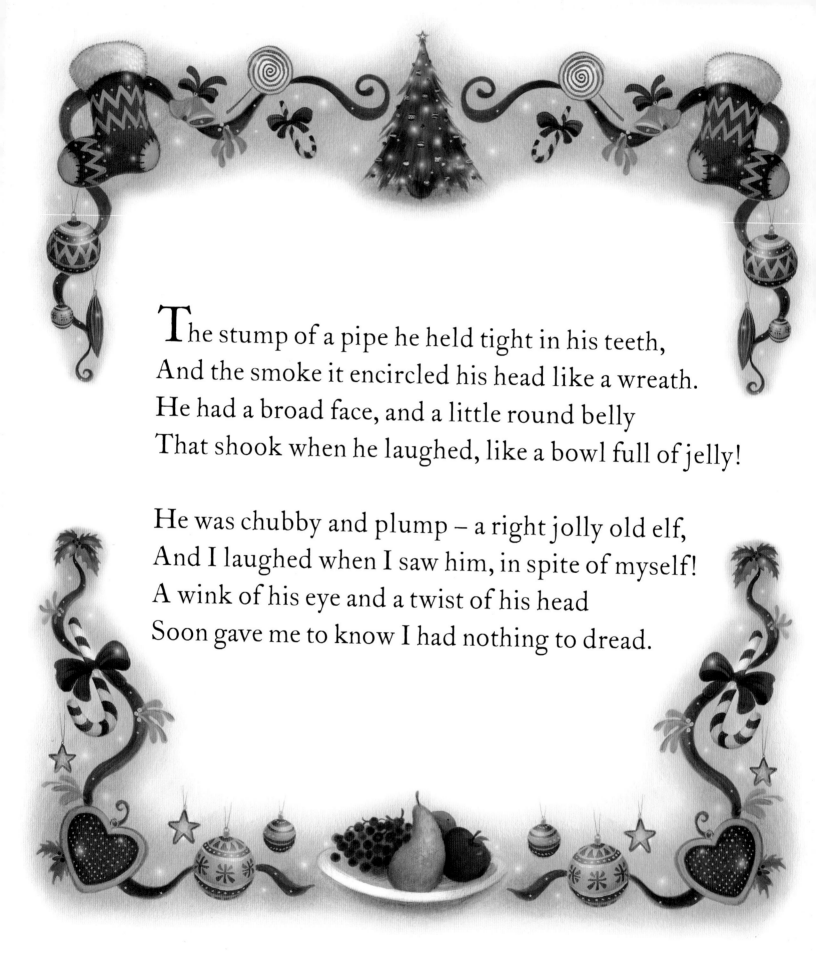

The stump of a pipe he held tight in his teeth,
And the smoke it encircled his head like a wreath.
He had a broad face, and a little round belly
That shook when he laughed, like a bowl full of jelly!

He was chubby and plump – a right jolly old elf,
And I laughed when I saw him, in spite of myself!
A wink of his eye and a twist of his head
Soon gave me to know I had nothing to dread.

He spoke not a word,
but went straight to his work,
And filled all the stockings;
then turned with a jerk,

And laying his finger aside of his nose,
And giving a nod, up the chimney he rose!

He sprang to his sleigh,
to his team gave a whistle,
And away they all flew

like the down of a thistle.
But I heard him exclaim
ere he drove out of sight . . .

"Merry Christmas to all,
and to all a good night!"

THE NIGHT BEFORE CHRISTMAS
A RED FOX BOOK 978 0 552 57467 9
Published in Great Britain by Picture Corgi,
an imprint of Random House Children's Publishers UK
A Random House Group Company
This edition published 2014

3 5 7 9 10 8 6 4

Written by Clement Clarke Moore
Illustrations copyright © Richard Johnson, 2014

Picture Corgi Books are published by Random House Children's Publishers UK,
61–63 Uxbridge Road, London W5 5SA
www.randomhousechildrens.co.uk
www.randomhouse.co.uk
Addresses for companies within The Random House Group Limited can be found at:
www.randomhouse.co.uk/offices.htm

THE RANDOM HOUSE GROUP Limited Reg. No. 954009
A CIP catalogue record for this book is available from the British Library.
Printed in China